SEE ME PLAY

Paul Meisel

I Like to Read®

HOLIDAY HOUSE • NEW YORK

HOLIDAY HOUSE is registered in the U.S. Patent and Trademark Office.

Printed and bound in October 2018 at Tien Wah Press, Johor Bahru, Johor, Malaysia.

Artwork was created with pen and ink with watercolor and acrylic on Strathmore paper and digital tools.

www.holidayhouse.com

First Edition

1 3 5 7 9 10 8 6 4 2

Library of Congress Cataloging-in-Publication Data

Names: Meisel, Paul, author, illustrator.

Title: See me play / Paul Meisel.

Description: First edition. | New York : Holiday House, [2019] | Series:
I like to read | Summary: In this easy-to-read book, a playful pack of dogs
chase a ball that is caught by a bird, a whale, and a lion.

Identifiers: LCCN 2018024183 | ISBN 9780823438327 (hardcover)

Subjects: | CYAC: Play—Fiction. | Dogs—Fiction. | Animals—Fiction.

Classification: LCC PZ7.M5158752 Sdv 2019 | DDC [E]--dc23 LC record available at https://lccn.loc.gov/2018024183

I see the ball.

I see the ball.

FOR PETE AND LIZ—AND RILEY!

The ball is fast.

The ball is wet.

The bird wants the ball.

The bird has the ball.

The bird drops the ball.

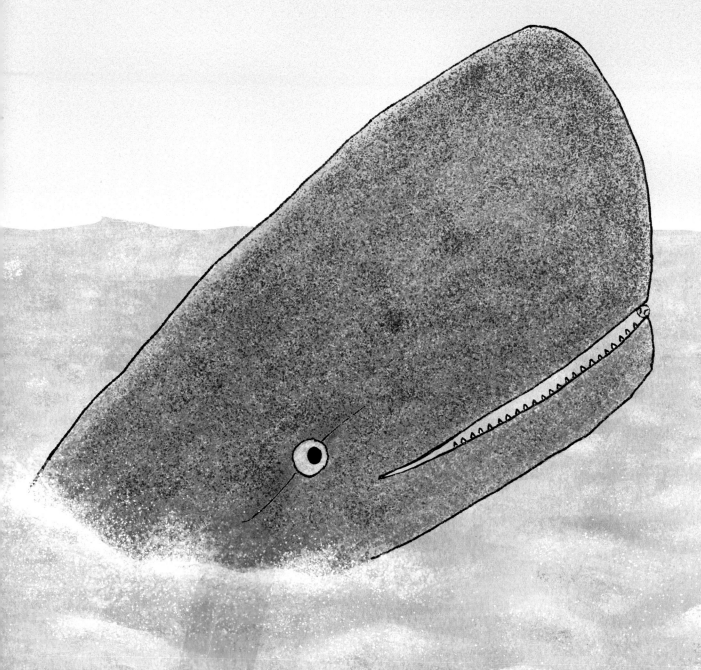

The whale has the ball.

The ball is going.

The lion has the ball.

I see a stick.